Lii Yiiboo Nayaapiwak lii Swer

L'ALFABET DI MICHIF

Owls See Clearly at Night

A MICHIF ALPHABET

JULIE FLETT

SIMPLY READ BOOKS

Introduction

Languages are precious; they capture the very essence of a culture. The exceptional night-sight of owls is akin to the insight that language offers in understanding a culture.

The Métis culture, a mix of First Nations (mostly the Cree and Ojibwe peoples) and European (mostly the French and Scots peoples), has gone through many transformations since it began. This mingling of cultures resulted in the Michif language that is a unique blend of Cree (Nēhiyawēwin) and French (Français) with some Saulteaux dialect of Ojibwe (Nakawēmowin; Anishinaabemowin). In its own way, the Michif language, with its Red River and buffalo-hunting roots, records the transformations of the Métis culture.

Michif was once spoken by thousands of people across the Prairies of Canada and the Northern US. It is now spoken in pockets of Manitoba, Saskatchewan, North Dakota, Alberta, Montana, and by other Métis communities scattered across North America. Michif is highly endangered, as are the unique Métis dialects of other languages traditionally spoken by Métis people, and could disappear within a generation. At one time, not only did many Métis people speak Michif, it was the norm to be multilingual. Some Elders still speak one or more traditional heritage languages in addition to English. Today most of the younger Métis are monolingual English speakers, but there has been a recent resurgence in interest in learning Michif and other Métis languages.

Michif, like all languages, was originally only a spoken language, not a written one. When Michif speakers began to record the language early on, they used a number of different ways to represent the sounds of their language and the spelling they used varied considerably. Recently, some of those working together to revitalize the language have realized that the letters q and x do not really represent sounds heard in Michif, so we will not see these letters in any Michif words (nor in this book). As well, whole sentences can quite often be expressed in one word in Michif, whereas in English this requires two or more. Commands are marked with an exclamation mark as in English. For pronunciation of the words, please refer to the guide at the back.

A

Atayookee!

Tell a story!

B

Li Bafloo

Buffalo

C

Lii Chiiraañ

Northern Lights

D Diloo
Water

E

Li Eenikooñs

Ant

F

Li Fezaañ

Pheasant

G

La Galet

Bannock

H

La Haruzh

Red Willow

I

Itohteew

He/she goes

J

La jig

Jig

K

Li Kanoo

Canoe

L

Lorzh
Barley

M Mawishow

He/she is picking berries

N

La Niizh

Snow

O Ohpaho!

Fly up! Fly away!

P

La Pwii

Rain

R

La Rooz Di No Piyii

Wild Rose

S Li Siiroo
Syrup

T

Taanshi

Hello

U

Lii Suyii Muu

Moccasins

V

Li Vyaloñ

Fiddle

W

Waapan

It is dawn

Y

Yootin

Windy

Z

Lii Zyeu

Eyes

Vowel Pronunciation Guide

	Michif example	English closest approximation	Notes
a	Atayookee, galet	'a' in *father*	
aa	Aachimo, kayaash	'aw' in *saw*	
i	Itohteew, yootin	'I' in *pit*	
ii	Chiiraañ, lii	'ee' in *bee*	
e	En, fleshii	'e' in *bet*	
ee	Eenikooñs, itweew	'ay' in *pay*	
o	Ohpahow, lorzh	'o' in *cot* or 'u' in *cut*	*The pronunciation of 'o' can change somewhat depending on what sounds come around it.*
oo	Poo, diloo	'oa' in *coat*	
u	Haruzh, rugaru	'u' in *lute*	*"U and "uu" are included here, but it is not clear yet whether there is actually both "o/oo" and "u/uu" in Michif or just one basic vowel sound. Future linguistic research will tell.*
uu	Muu, luu	'oo' in *moo* (the sound a cow makes)	
oe	Soer, doktoer	n/a in English	
eu	Zyeu, feu	n/a in English	
añ	fezaañ, tañt	n/a in English	*Vowels immediately followed by a ñ are nasalized. This means air passes both through your mouth and your nose, not just your mouth. English does not have a true distinction between nasal and non-nasal vowels. At the same time, you can hear a slightly nasal vowel in the word 'bank' that you do not when you say 'back'. Note, however, that Michif vowels are usually more strongly nasalized than this.*
aeñ	saeñcheur, aeñ	n/a in English	
oñ	Vyaloñ, Moñ	n/a in English	
iñ	Ohiñ, chiiñ	n/a in English	

Credits: Grace Zoldy, Heather Souter and Nicole Rosen

Consonant Pronunciation Guide

	Michif example	English closest approximation	Notes
p	Pwii, piyii	'p' in *span*	
b	Bafloo, barb	Like English 'b'	
hp	Ohpaho, pahpi	n/a	*Like it's written, with a puff of air (an 'h' sound) before the p.*
t	Tart, yootin, taanshi	't' in *stack*	
d	Diloo, Taandee	Like an English 'd'	
ht	Itohteew, teehtapi	n/a	*Like it's written, with a puff of air (an 'h' sound) before the t.*
k	Kanoo, shiikahoo	'k' in *skip*	
g	Galet, magazaeñ	Like an English 'g'	
hk	Ahkoshiw, teepiyaahk	n/a	*Like it's written, with a puff of air (an 'h' sound) before the k.*
f	Fezaañ, Michif	Like an English 'f'	
v	Vyaloñ, avik	Like an English 'v'	
s	Siiroo, rasad	Like an English 's'	
z	Zyeu, rooz	Like an English 'z'	
sh	Shar, kiishta	Like the 'sh' in *ship*	
zh	zhveu, niizh	Like the 's' in *treasure*	
h	Haruzh, peehin	Like an English 'h'	
ch	Chiikaha, wiichihin	'ch' in *cheap*	
hch	Ohchi	'sch' of *borscht*	*Usually pronounced 'shch'*
j	jis, jig	'j' in *jog*	
m	mawishow, lom	Like an English 'm'	
n	nayaapiwak, niizh, miina	Like an English 'n'	
l	lorzh, zhalii	Like an English 'l'	
r	rooz, doktoer	n/a in English	*The 'r' is most often rolled, unlike in English.*
w	Waapan, awa	Like an English 'w'	
y	Yootin, suyii	'y' in *youth*	

Credits: Grace (Ledoux) Zoldy, Heather Souter, and Nicole Rosen

Author's Note

THIS BOOK WOULD NOT HAVE BEEN possible without the contributions of Elder Grace (Ledoux) Zoldy, Métis Elder and fluent Michif speaker from Camperville, Manitoba; Métis language activist Heather Souter, MA, Michif language & linguistics, University of Lethbridge; and Dr. Nicole Rosen, Assistant Professor, Department of Modern Languages, University of Lethbridge. I also want to thank the following people for their care and support during the project, their second ears and eyes, counsel & warmth: Sonja Ahlers, Carla Bergman, Elaine Clare, Jeff Chute, Gwen Chute, Christine Corlett, my son Amiel Flett-Brown, my sister Leanne Flett-Kruger, my dad Clarence Flett, cousin Geraldine Flett-Horbas, uncle Len Flett, auntie Josephine Flett, Margaret Fogg, Kallie George, Lucie Lacaille, Iain Marrs, Robin Mitchell-Cranfield, Lorraine Muskego, Michelle Nahanee, Tasnim Nathoo, my publisher Dimiter Savoff, Windsor House School, and the Vancouver Public Library.

A special thanks to my mother, Shirley Kwong, who provided me with an enormous amount of emotional support during the making of this book. Sadly, she wasn't able to see this book be completed.

Thank you, Mom.

THIS BOOK IS DEDICATED TO my son Amiel, my little night-owl, for his love, curiosity, and inspiration; my niece Sage, who sewed me up a new heart just when I needed; my niece Autumn who draws the most inspiring owls out there; and to my grandparents Archie Flett and Annie Lavallee.

I'd also like to acknowledge the support of the First Peoples' Heritage, Language and Culture Council; Aboriginal Arts Development Awards for supporting the project.

All my relations
Kihchi-maarsii! Eekoshi!
(Thank-you very much! That's all!)

Resources

For anyone who would like to learn more about the Michif Language here are some useful resources:

The Gabriel Dumont Institute (GDI)
www.gdins.org/home.html
www.metismuseum.ca

Métis National Counsel
www.metisnation.ca

The Métis Culture and Heritage Resource Centre
www.metisresourcecentre.mb.ca

www.michifdictionary.org

BOOKS

La Lawng: Michif Peekishkwewin: The Heritage Language of the Canadian Métis, Vol. 2, Language Theory, edited by Lawrence Barkwell

La Lawng: Michif Peekishkwewin/The Canadian Michif Language Dictionary (Introductory Level), by Norman Fleury

Language of Our Own, A: The Genesis of Michif, the Mixed Cree-French Language of the Canadian Métis by Peter Bakker

Métis Legacy (Volume II): Michif Culture, Heritage, and Folkways, edited by Lawrence J. Barkwell, Leah Dorion and Audreen Hourie

The Michif Dictionary: Turtle Mountain Chippewa Cree by Patline Laverdure and Ida Rose Allard; edited by John C. Crawford

First published in 2010 by Simply Read Books
www.simplyreadbooks.com

Library and Archives Canada Cataloguing in Publication

Flett, Julie
        Lii yiiboo nayaapiwak lii swer : l'alfabet di Michif = Owls see clearly
at night : a Michif alphabet / Julie Flett.

Includes bibliographical references.
Text in Michif and English.
ISBN 978-1-897476-28-4

        1. Michif language–Alphabet. 2. Alphabet books.
I. Title. II. Title: Owls see clearly at night.

PM7895.M53F53 2010   497'.3   C2009-904015-8

We gratefully acknowledge for their financial support of our publishing
program the Canada Council for the Arts, the BC Arts Council, and the
Government of Canada through the Book Publishing Industry Development
Program (BPIDP).

Book design by Robin Mitchell-Cranfield for hundreds & thousands

10 9 8 7 6 5 4 3 2 1

Manufactured in China in January 2010 by C&C Offset Printing Co. Ltd.

Shenzhen, Guangdong Province

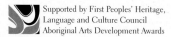

Supported by First Peoples' Heritage,
Language and Culture Council
Aboriginal Arts Development Awards